Hillsboro Public Library
Hillsboro, OR
A member of Washington County
COOPERATIVE LIBRARY SERVICES

Topic: Kindergarten and Friends   **Subtopic:** School Field Trip

Notes to Parents and Teachers:

The books your child reads at this level will have more of a storyline with details to discuss. Have children practice reading more fluently at this level. Take turns reading pages with your child so you can model what fluent reading sounds like.

REMEMBER: PRAISE IS A GREAT MOTIVATOR!

Here are some praise points for beginning readers:

- I love how you read that sentence so it sounded just like you were talking.
- Great job reading that sentence like a question!
- WOW! You read that page with such good expression!

Book Ends for the Reader!

Here are some reminders before reading the text:

- Use your eyes to follow the words in the story instead of pointing to each word.
- Read smoothly and with expression. Read like you are talking. Reread sections of the book to practice reading fluently.
- Look for interesting illustrations and words in the story.

Words to Know Before You Read

chair

dinosaur

map

movie

museum

skeleton

spikes

tickets

THE DINOSAUR MUSEUM

By
Hannah Ko
Illustrated by
Srimalie Bassani

Rourke
Educational Media
rourkeeducationalmedia.com

Mrs. Murphy's class is on a field trip.

They are at the dinosaur museum.

Mrs. Murphy points to a skeleton. "Who knows what dinosaur this is?" she asked.

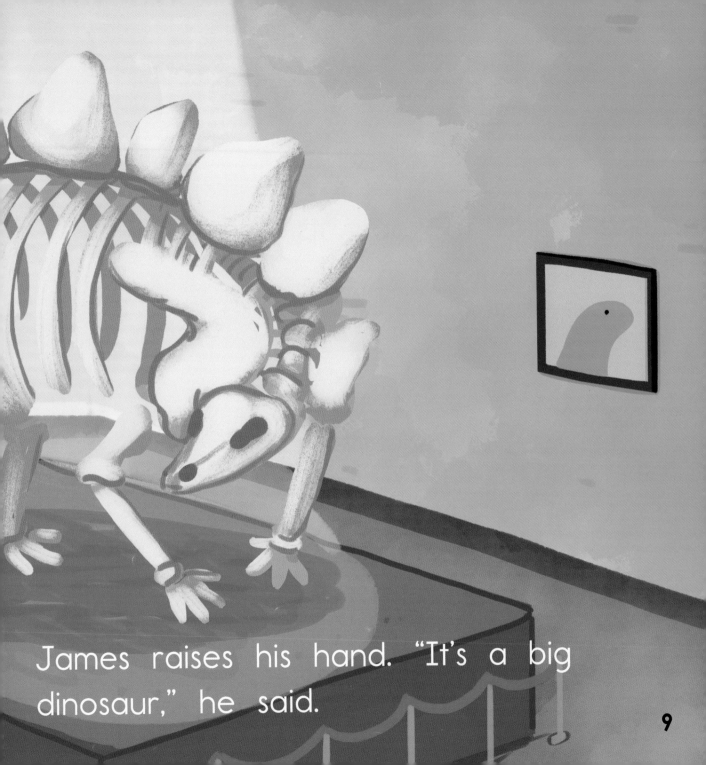

James raises his hand. "It's a big dinosaur," he said.

"She wants to know its name," Tim laughs.

"It is a stegosaurus. Look at the spikes on its tail!" said James.

Mrs. Murphy looks at the map. "It's time to watch the 3D movie," she said.

Everyone goes to the theater. The movie is about dangerous dinosaurs.

"Is the movie scary?" asked James.
"Don't worry, James. You will be okay,"
Mrs. Murphy said.

14

"Ha-ha, you are a coward. I am brave! I'm not scared!" Tim said.

Mrs. Murphy hands out the 3D glasses.

"Take your seats. The movie will start soon," said Mrs. Murphy.

The movie comes to an end.
James is shaking.

"I was so scared the dinosaur was going to eat me!" said Tim.

Tim helps James out of his chair.

20

"I'm sorry I called you a coward." said Tim. "That's okay," said James.

Book Ends for the Reader

I know...

1. Why is Mrs. Murphy's class at the dinosaur museum?

2. Why did Tim laugh at James?

3. Why was James shaking?

I think ...

1. Have you ever been to a dinosaur museum?

2. What kind of dinosaurs can you think of?

3. Have you ever watched a 3D movie?

Book Ends for the Reader

What happened in this book?

Look at each picture and talk about what happened in the story.

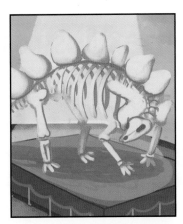

About the Author

Hannah Ko has been a teacher for many years. She lives with her husband and child in Korea.
Her favorite part about children's books is imagination. She likes the beautiful sunshine and also enjoys scuba diving in tropical oceans.

About the Illustrator

Since Srimalie was a child her mother gave her the passion for drawing and painting, and she had always encouraged her artistic expression. Her work is always full of surprises. It's difficult to remove her from her writing desk, where she keeps a stack of books, pages, tea cups of many colors and also amuses her fat cat.

33614080635393

Library of Congress PCN Data

The Dinosaur Museum / Hannah Ko

ISBN 978-1-68342-736-0 (hard cover)(alk. paper)
ISBN 978-1-68342-788-9 (soft cover)
ISBN 978-1-68342-840-4 (e-Book)
Library of Congress Control Number: 2017935451

Rourke Educational Media
Printed in the United States of America, North Mankato, Minnesota

© 2018 Rourke Educational Media

All rights reserved. No part of this book may be reproduced or utilized in any form or by any means, electronic or mechanical including photocopying, recording, or by any information storage and retrieval system without permission in writing from the publisher.

www.rourkeeducationalmedia.com

Edited by: Debra Ankiel
Art direction and layout by: Rhea Magaro-Wallace
Cover and interior Illustrations by: Srimalie Bassani